Dear Parent:
Your child's love of reading starts here!

Every child learns to read in a different way and at his or her own speed. Some go back and forth between reading levels and read favorite books again and again. Others read through each level in order. You can help your young reader improve and become more confident by encouraging his or her own interests and abilities. From books your child reads with you to the first books he or she reads alone, there are I Can Read Books for every stage of reading:

SHARED READING
Basic language, word repetition, and whimsical illustrations, ideal for sharing with your emergent reader

BEGINNING READING
Short sentences, familiar words, and simple concepts for children eager to read on their own

READING WITH HELP
Engaging stories, longer sentences, and language play for developing readers

READING ALONE
Complex plots, challenging vocabulary, and high-interest topics for the independent reader

ADVANCED READING
Short paragraphs, chapters, and exciting themes for the perfect bridge to chapter books

I Can Read Books have introd _____ ding since 1957. Featuring award-winni _____ a fabulous cast of beloved characters _____ set the standard for beginning readers.

A lifetime of discovery begins with the magical words "I Can Read!"

Visit www.icanread.com for information
on enriching your child's reading experience.

ALVIN
AND
THE CHIPMUNKS
THE SQUEAKQUEL

Alvin and the Chipmunks: The Squeakquel: Meet the 'Munks
"Alvin and the Chipmunks: the Squeakquel" Motion Picture © 2009 Twentieth Century Fox Film Corporation and Regency Entertainment
(USA), Inc. in the U.S. only; © 2009 Twentieth Century Fox Film Corporation and Monarchy Enterprises S.a.r.l. in all other territories.
Alvin and the Chipmunks, The Chipettes and Characters TM & © 2009 Bagdasarian Productions, LLC. All rights reserved.
Printed in the United States of America.

Library of Congress catalog card number: 2009935248
ISBN 978-0-06-184566-6

10 11 12 13   LP/WOR   10 9 8 7 6   ❖   First Edition

FOX 2000 PICTURES AND REGENCY ENTERPRISES PRESENT A BAGDASARIAN COMPANY PRODUCTION A BETTY THOMAS FILM "ALVIN AND THE CHIPMUNKS: THE SQUEAKQU
ZACH LEVI DAVID CROSS AND JASON LEE AND JUSTIN LONG MATTHEW GRAY GUBLER JESSE McCARTNEY AMY POEHLER ANNA FARIS CHRISTINA APPLEGATE
COSTUME DESIGNER ALEXANDRA WELKER MUSIC PRODUCER ALI DEE THEODORE MUSIC SUPERVISOR JULIANNE JORDAN MUSIC BY DAVID NEWMAN ANIMATION SUPERVISOR CHRIS BAILEY FILM EDITOR MATTHEW FRIEDMAN
PRODUCTION DESIGNER MARCIA HINDS DIRECTOR OF PHOTOGRAPHY ANTHONY B. RICHMOND, ASC/BSC EXECUTIVE PRODUCERS KAREN ROSENFELT ARNON MILCHAN MICHELE IMPERATO STABILE STEVE WATERMAN
PRODUCED BY JANICE KARMAN ROSS BAGDASARIAN "ALVIN AND THE CHIPMUNKS" CREATED BY ROSS BAGDASARIAN SCREENPLAY BY WILL McROBB AND CHRIS VISCARDI DIRECTED BY BETTY THOMAS

SOUNDTRACK ON RHINO [DOLBY]   www.munkyourself.com

Alvin and the Chipmunks, the Chipettes and Characters
TM & © 2009 Bagdasarian Productions, LLC. All Rights Reserved.
© 2009 Twentieth Century Fox Film Corporation. All Rights Reserved.

ALVIN AND THE CHIPMUNKS™
THE SQUEAKQUEL

Meet the 'Munks

Adapted by Susan Hill Long

HARPER

An Imprint of HarperCollinsPublishers

Alvin, Simon, and Theodore
were no ordinary chipmunks.
They knew how to sing.
They knew how to dance.
And they knew how to rock and roll.

So when their school

had a singing contest,

Alvin was sure they'd win.

Alvin was so sure The Chipmunks

would win the contest

that he played football

with his cool new friends

instead of practicing

with his brothers.

Simon wasn't sure they'd win.
"I'm kind of a big picture guy,"
said Simon.

"And the big picture tells me
you can't win if you don't practice,"
he said.

12

Theodore was sure

they would lose the contest.

"It's one for all

and three for one," said Theodore.

"Without Alvin,

we just aren't The Chipmunks!"

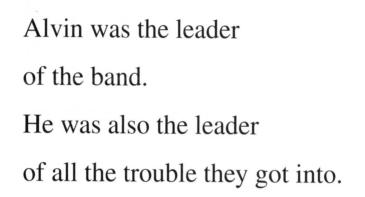

Alvin was the leader
of the band.

He was also the leader
of all the trouble they got into.

Now The Chipmunks
were in deep trouble.

Dave couldn't help.

He was far away in a hospital bed.

He couldn't move!

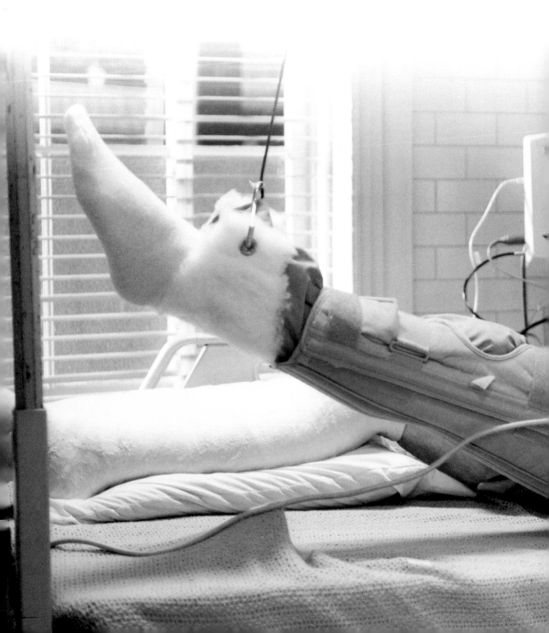

"What's going on, guys?"

Dave wondered.

He missed The Chipmunks,

but they told him they were okay.

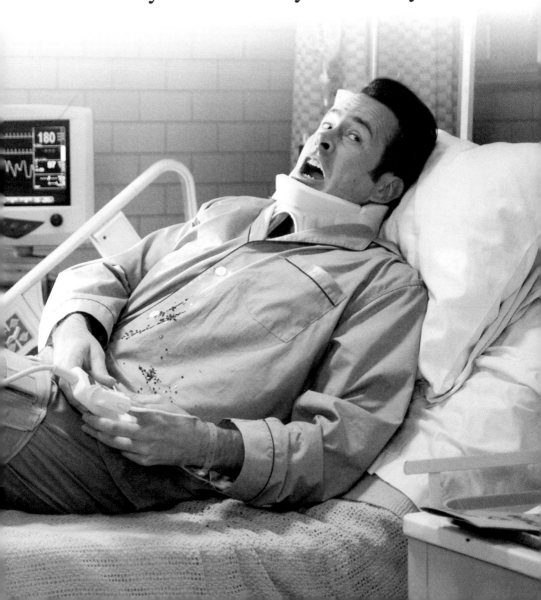

Ian, their old manager, had worked
with Alvin, Simon, and Theodore
when they first started singing.
But Ian only cared about money,
so The Chipmunks left him.
"I lost everything," said Ian.
"I just hope and pray that
somewhere out there
are other animals
who can sing and dance."

One day,

three of The Chipmunks' biggest fans

came to Los Angeles.

"We made it, girls," said Brittany.

"I can't believe we're really here!"

Brittany, Eleanor, and Jeanette

were no ordinary fans.

They were singers.

They were dancers.

They were The Chipettes!

Brittany was the group's leader.

She led her sisters right

to the basement of Jett Records

where Ian now lived.

"He made The Chipmunks famous,"

she said.

"He can make us stars, too!"

Jeanette wasn't sure of anything.

"I'm Jeanette," she said.

"Although I feel more like an Olivia, or an Emily . . ."

Eleanor wasn't thinking

about singing at all.

She only wanted to know one thing—

"When do you think

we can meet The Chipmunks?"

It was time for the contest.

Would Alvin get back

from the football game in time

to go onstage with The Chipmunks?

Or would The Chipettes

sing and win it all?

All the fans were gathered
at the school.

Even Dave made it.

The Chipettes began to sing.

Then The Chipmunks joined in.

And when the two groups

performed together,

they were unbeatable!